WELCOME TO
PASSPORT TO READING
A beginning reader's ticket to a brand-new world!

Every book in this program is designed to build read-along and read-alone skills, level by level, through engaging and enriching stories. As the reader turns each page, he or she will become more confident with new vocabulary, sight words, and comprehension.

These PASSPORT TO READING levels will help you choose the perfect book for every reader.

READING TOGETHER
Read short words in simple sentence structures together to begin a reader's journey.

READING OUT LOUD
Encourage developing readers to sound out words in more complex stories with simple vocabulary.

READING INDEPENDENTLY
Newly independent readers gain confidence reading more complex sentences with higher word counts.

READY TO READ MORE
Readers prepare for chapter books with fewer illustrations and longer paragraphs.

This book features sight words from the educator-supported Dolch Sight Words List. This encourages the reader to recognize commonly used vocabulary words, increasing reading speed and fluency.

For more information, please visit passporttoreadingbooks.com.

Enjoy the journey!

Little, Brown and Company

Hachette Book Group
1290 Avenue of the Americas, New York, NY 10104
Visit our website at lb-kids.com

Little, Brown and Company is a division of Hachette Book Group, Inc.
The Little, Brown name and logo are trademarks of Hachette Book Group, Inc.

The publisher is not responsible for websites (or their content) that are not owned by the publisher.

First Edition: September 2014

Library of Congress Control Number: 2014941979

ISBN 978-0-316-28230-7

10 9 8 7

CW

Printed in the United States of America

Passport to Reading titles are leveled by independent reviewers applying the standards developed by Irene Fountas and Gay Su Pinnell in *Matching Books to Readers: Using Leveled Books in Guided Reading*, Heinemann, 1999.

Licensed By:

MEET THE
PRINCESS OF FRIENDSHIP

Adapted by Lucy Rosen

Based on the episodes
"Twilight's Kingdom – Parts 1 and 2"
written by Meghan McCarthy

LITTLE, BROWN AND COMPANY
New York   Boston

Attention, My Little Pony fans! Look for these words when you read this book. Can you spot them all?

princess

moon

castle

throne

Princess Twilight Sparkle is the
newest princess in Equestria.

Twilight Sparkle was
not always a princess.
She came to Ponyville
to learn about friendship
and to study magic.

One day, Twilight Sparkle
used magic to help her friends.
She cast a brand-new spell
and saved the day.

Nopony had ever created new magic
with the power of friendship before!

Princess Celestia was so proud.
She had always known
that Twilight Sparkle
was a very special pony.

"Now you are ready to fulfill
your destiny," Princess Celestia
told Twilight Sparkle.

A beam of light swirled
around Twilight Sparkle.
When it cleared,
Twilight Sparkle looked different.
She was an Alicorn,
a Unicorn with wings!

"You look like a princess,"
Fluttershy whispered.
"Now she is one,"
said Princess Celestia.

That is how Princess Twilight
became one of the four leaders
of Equestria.

Together, these leaders
make sure the ponies
live together in peace
and harmony.

Princess Celestia lives in Canterlot
with her sister, Princess Luna.
They used to fight,
but now they are as close as can be.

They make the sun and moon
rise and set each day.

Princess Cadance
rules the Crystal Empire.
She is married to Shining Armor.
He is Princess Twilight's brother!

Princess Twilight is proud to lead
with the other royal ponies.
But she is not sure what
it means to be a princess.

Princess Twilight does not have
a special job like the others.
She does not have a castle
like the others.
All she does is smile and wave.

One day, an evil creature
comes to Equestria.
It is Tirek.
He is out to steal
everypony's magic!

Nopony can stop him,

not even the other princesses.

But Princess Twilight has a plan.

She knows there is something
even stronger than Tirek.
It is the power of friendship!

Princess Twilight gathers her friends.
Rainbow Dash, Pinkie Pie,
Rarity, Applejack, and
Fluttershy give all their
might to defeat the evil villain.

With the help of her friends,
Princess Twilight releases
rainbow power.

A flash of light
blinds the ponies.
When they open their eyes,
they cannot believe what they see!

Where Tirek once stood,
there is now a beautiful castle.
"It belongs to you, Princess Twilight,"
says Princess Celestia.

The friends are in awe.

Inside the castle,

there are six thrones,

one for each pony.

There is even a throne for Spike!

"Now do you understand
what you are meant to do
as a princess?"
asks Princess Celestia.

Princess Twilight smiles.

"Yes," she says.

"I am meant to spread
the magic of friendship
all across Equestria."

"That makes you
the princess of friendship,"
says Princess Celestia.

At last, Princess Twilight
knows her destiny.
And what is the princess of friendship
without her friends by her side?